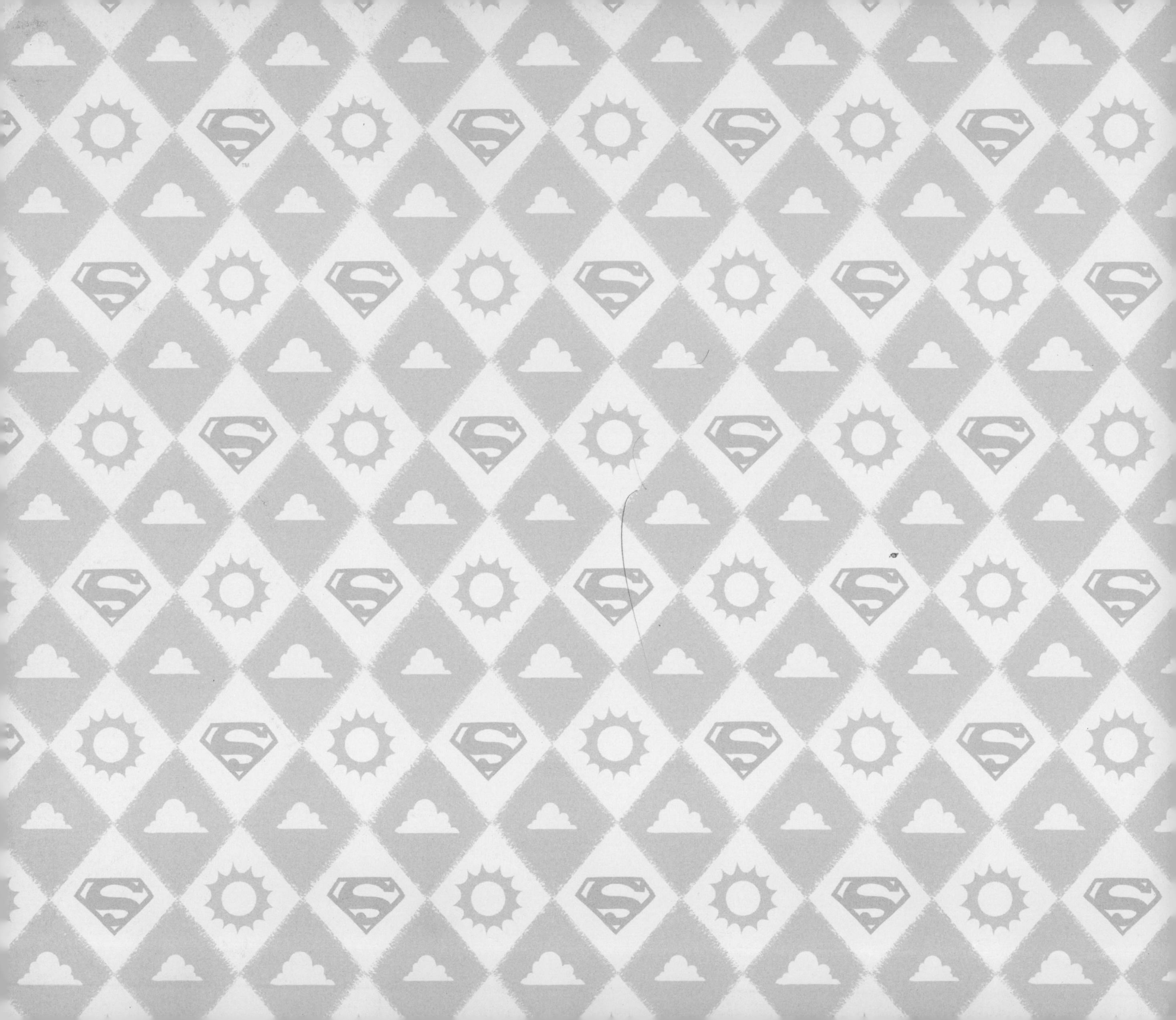

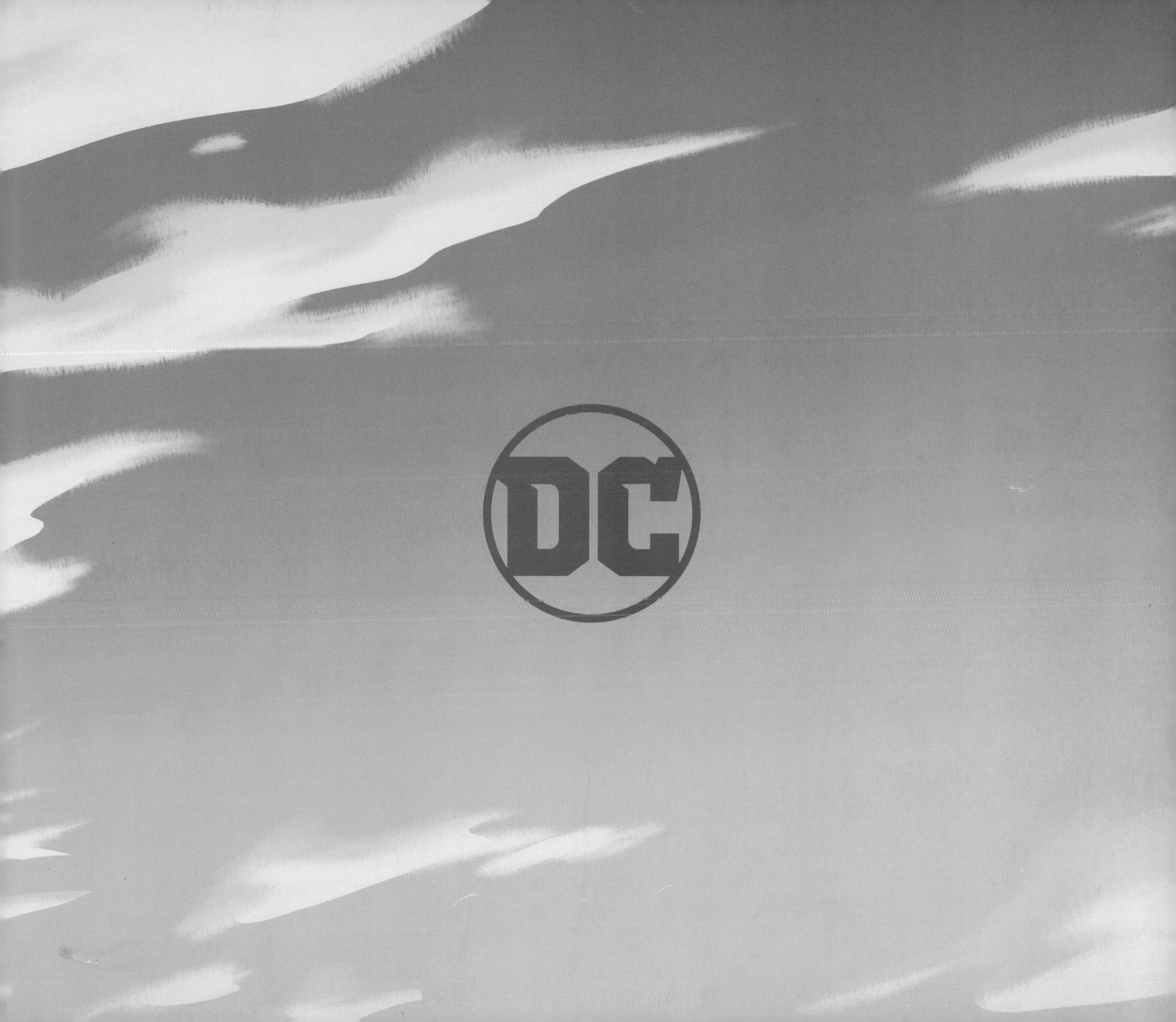
DC

Good Morning, Superman is published by
Capstone Young Readers
a Capstone imprint
1710 Roe Crest Drive
North Mankato, Minnesota 56003
www.mycapstone.com

STAR37926

Cataloging-in-Publication Data is available on the
Library of Congress website.

ISBN: 978-1-62370-850-4 (jacketed hardcover)
ISBN: 978-1-62370-851-1 (eBook pdf)

Jacket and book design by Bob Lentz

Printed and bound in China.
009974S17

words by **MICHAEL DAHL**

pictures by **OMAR LOZANO**

GOOD MORNING, SUPERMAN™

Superman created by
JERRY SIEGEL and **JOE SHUSTER**
by special arrangement with the Jerry Siegel family

CAPSTONE YOUNG READERS
a Capstone imprint

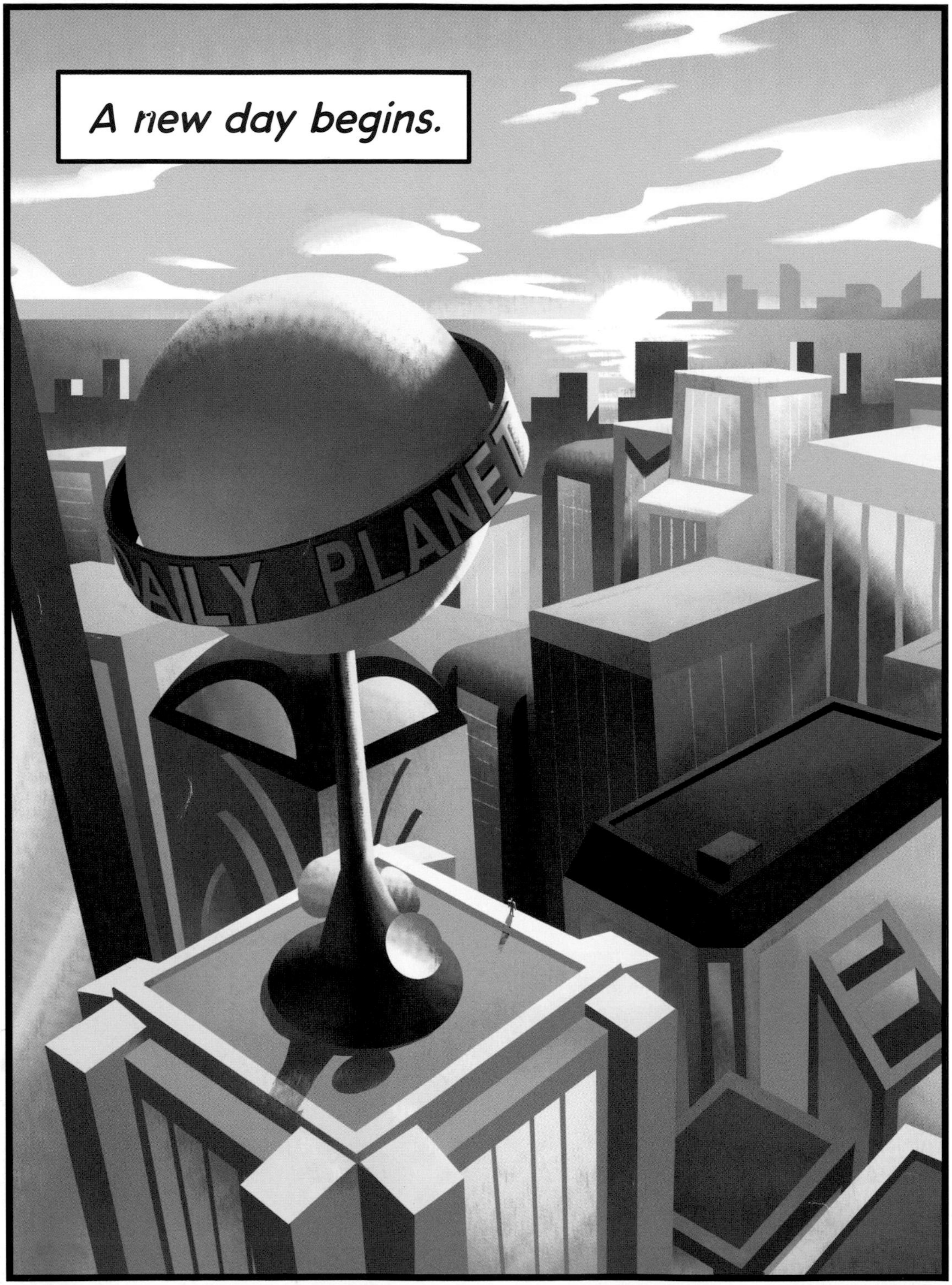
A new day begins.

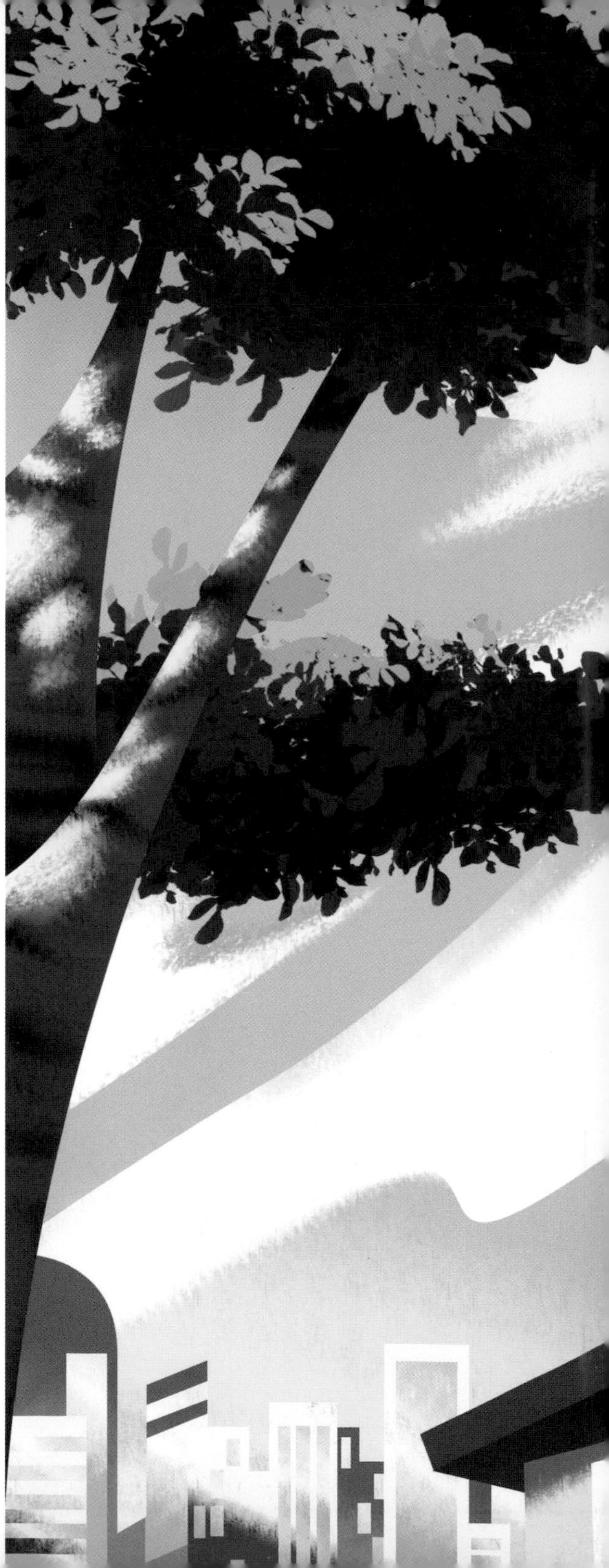

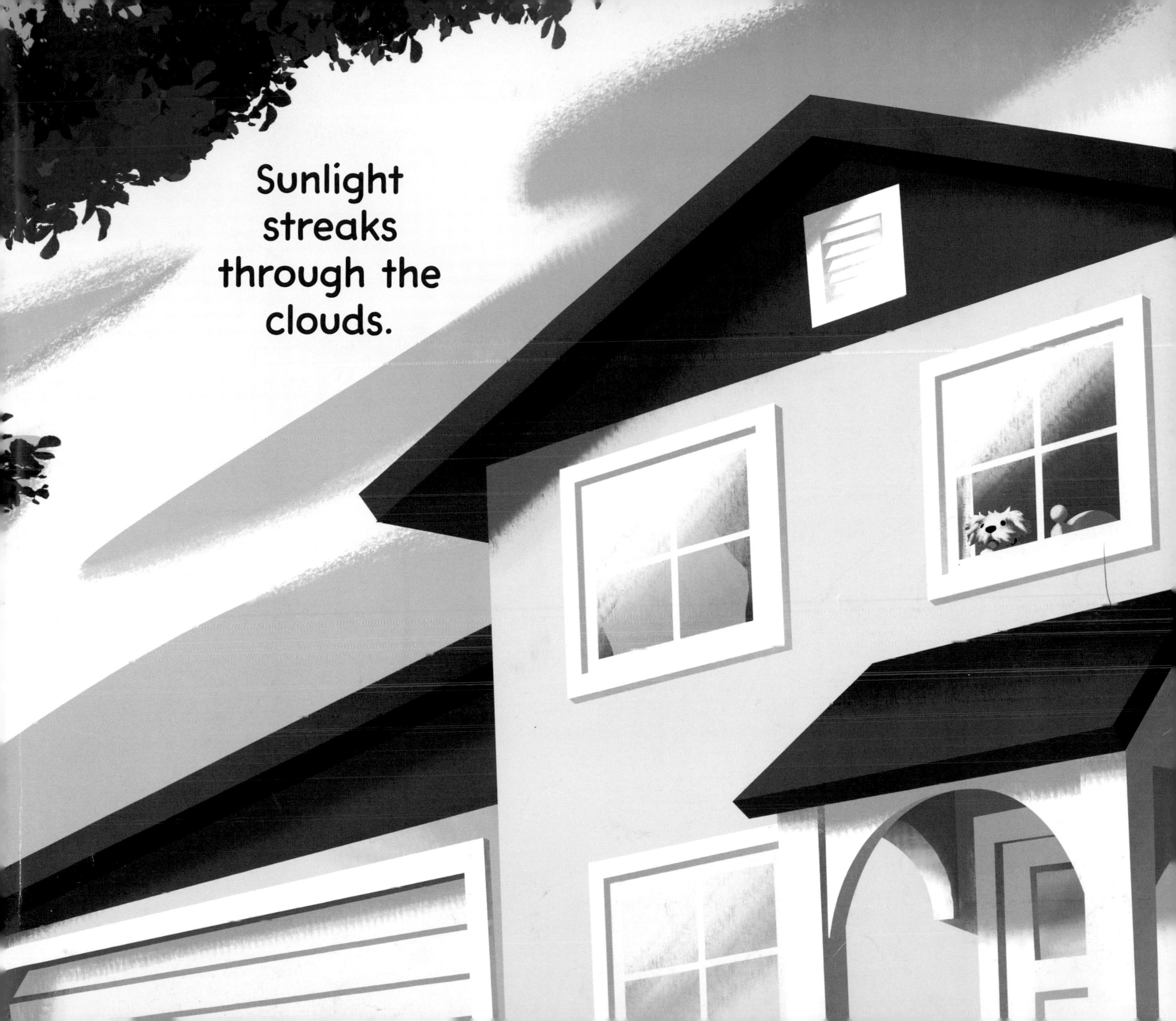

Sunlight streaks through the clouds.

A bird chirps.

A plane soars overhead.

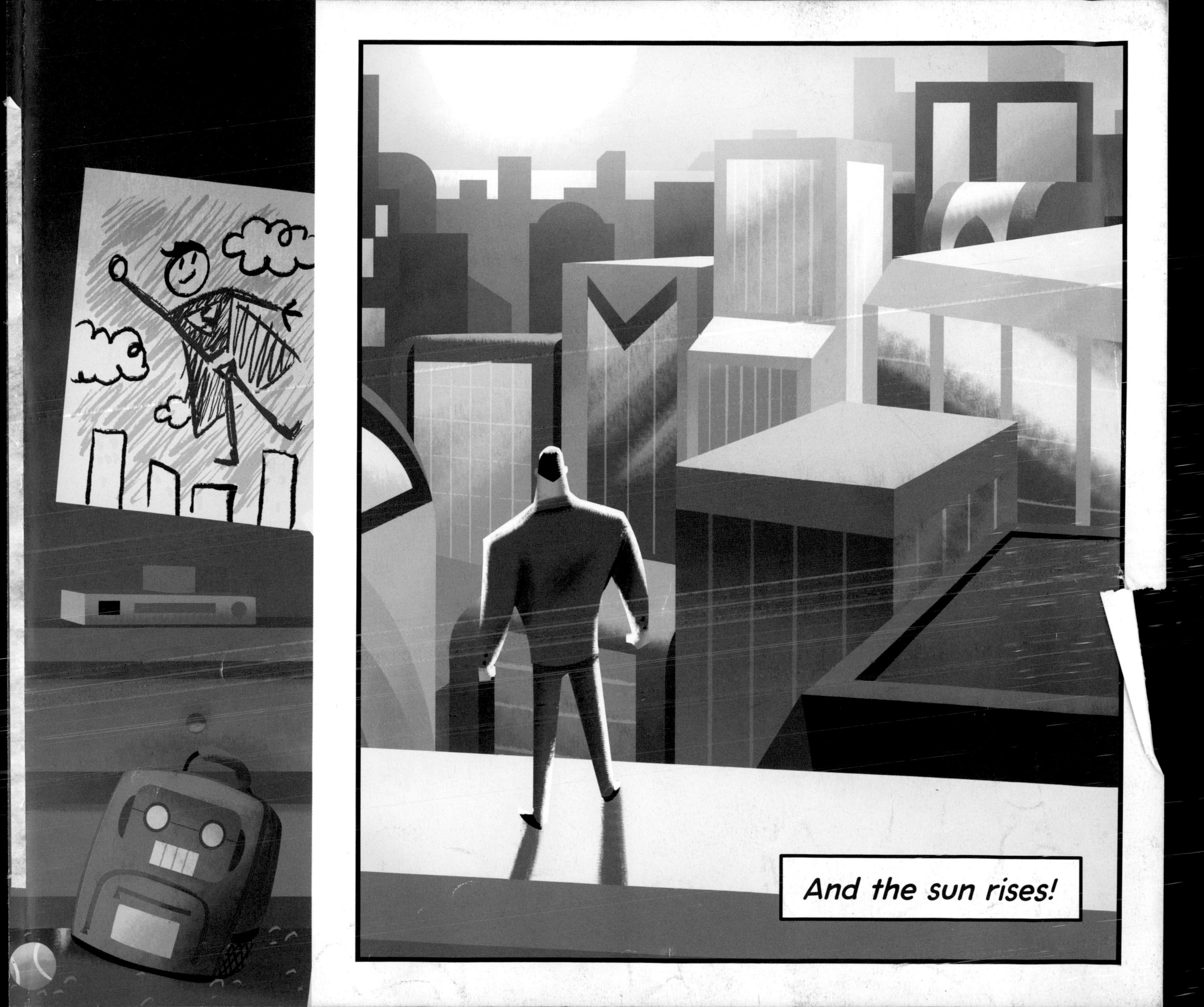
And the sun rises!

Powerful golden rays
stream down . . .

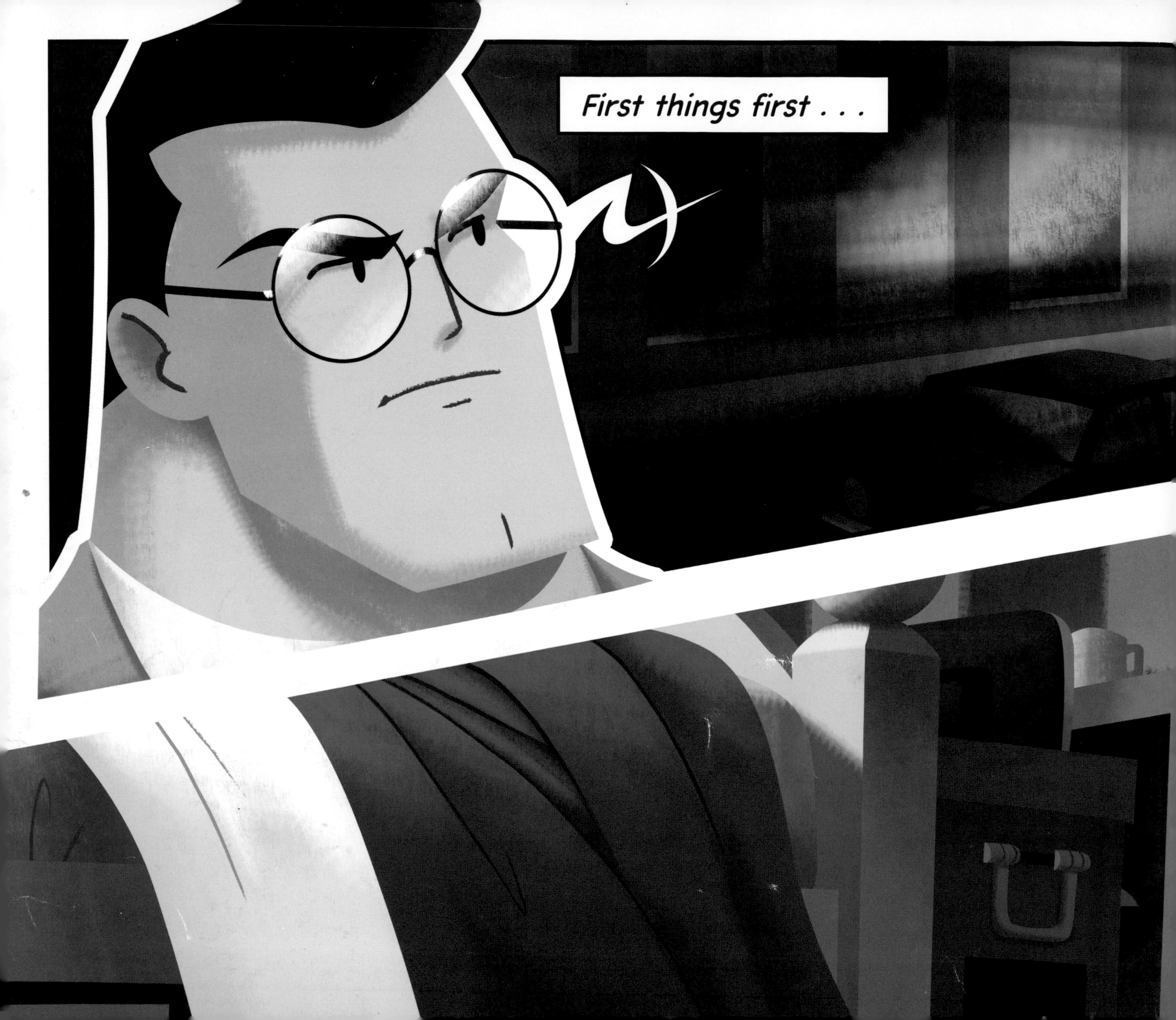
First things first . . .

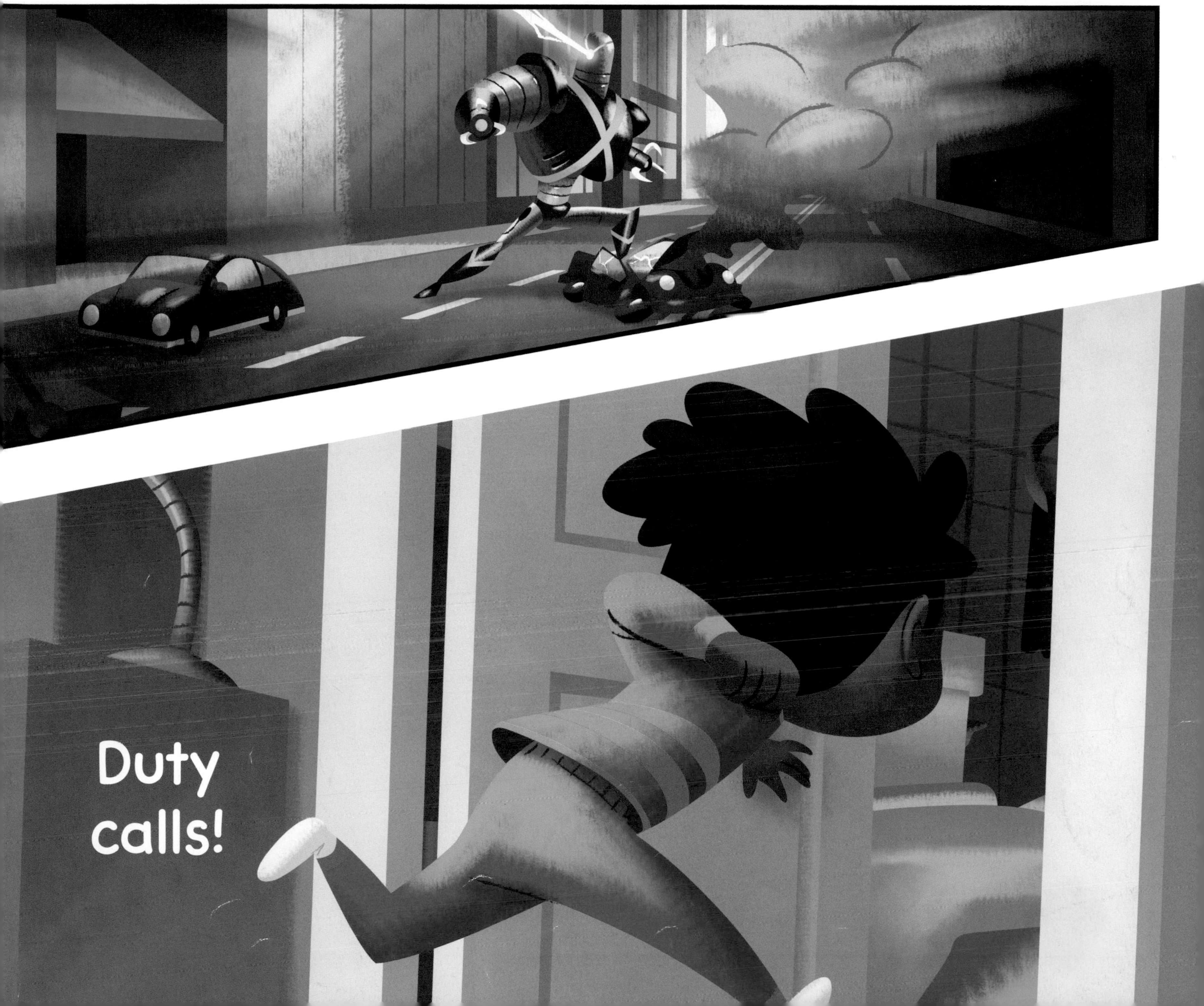
Duty calls!

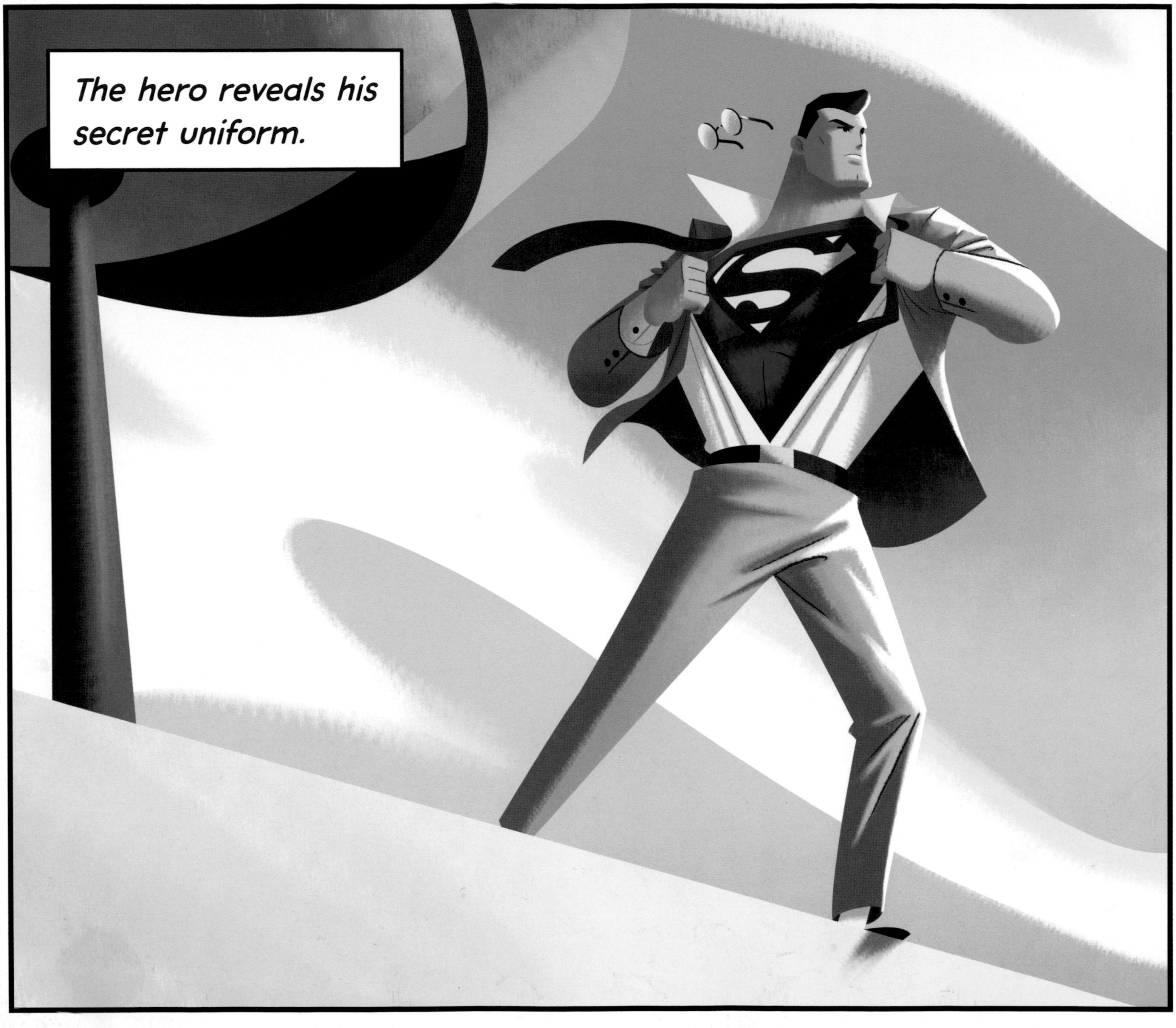
The hero reveals his secret uniform.

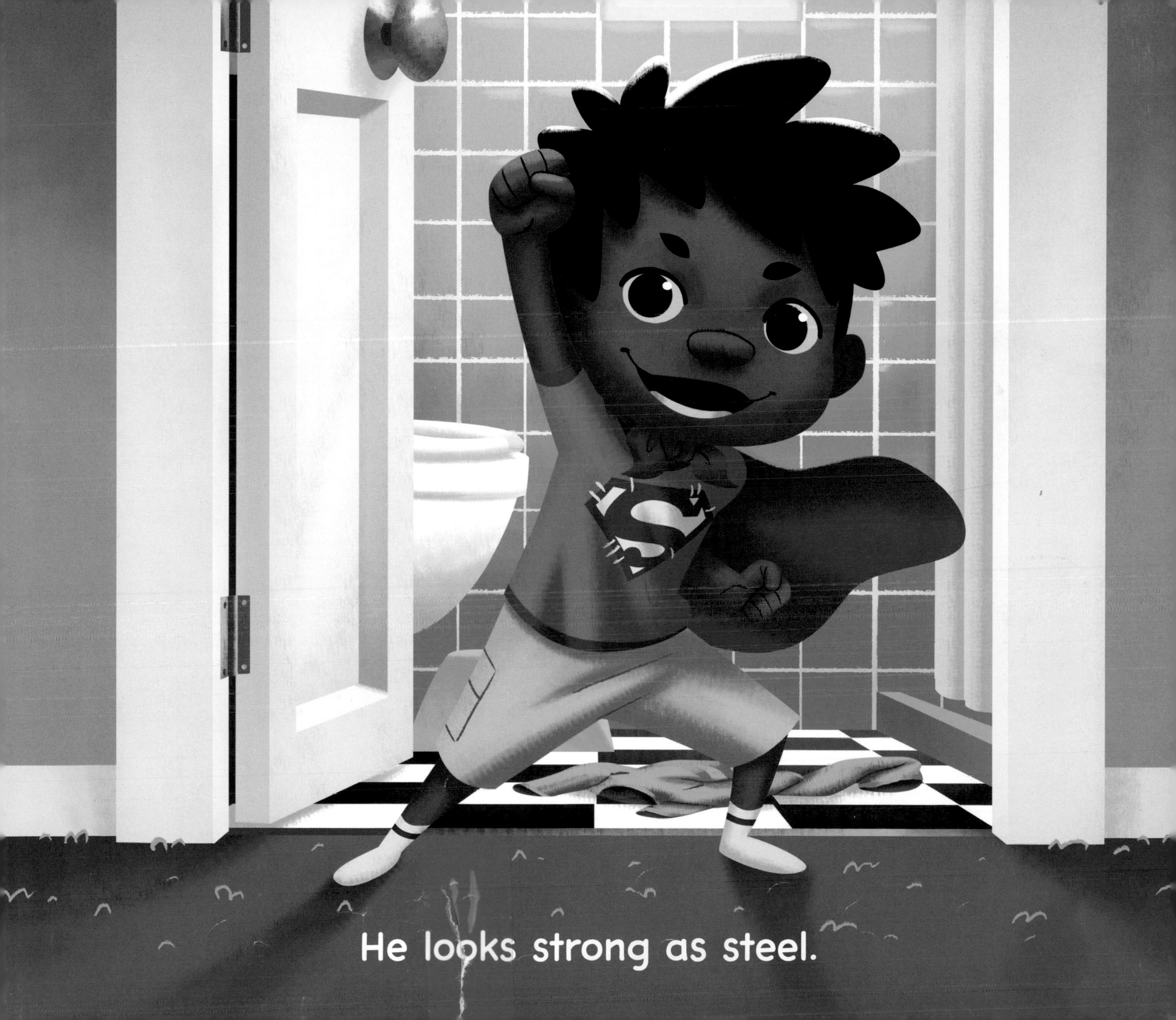

He looks strong as steel.

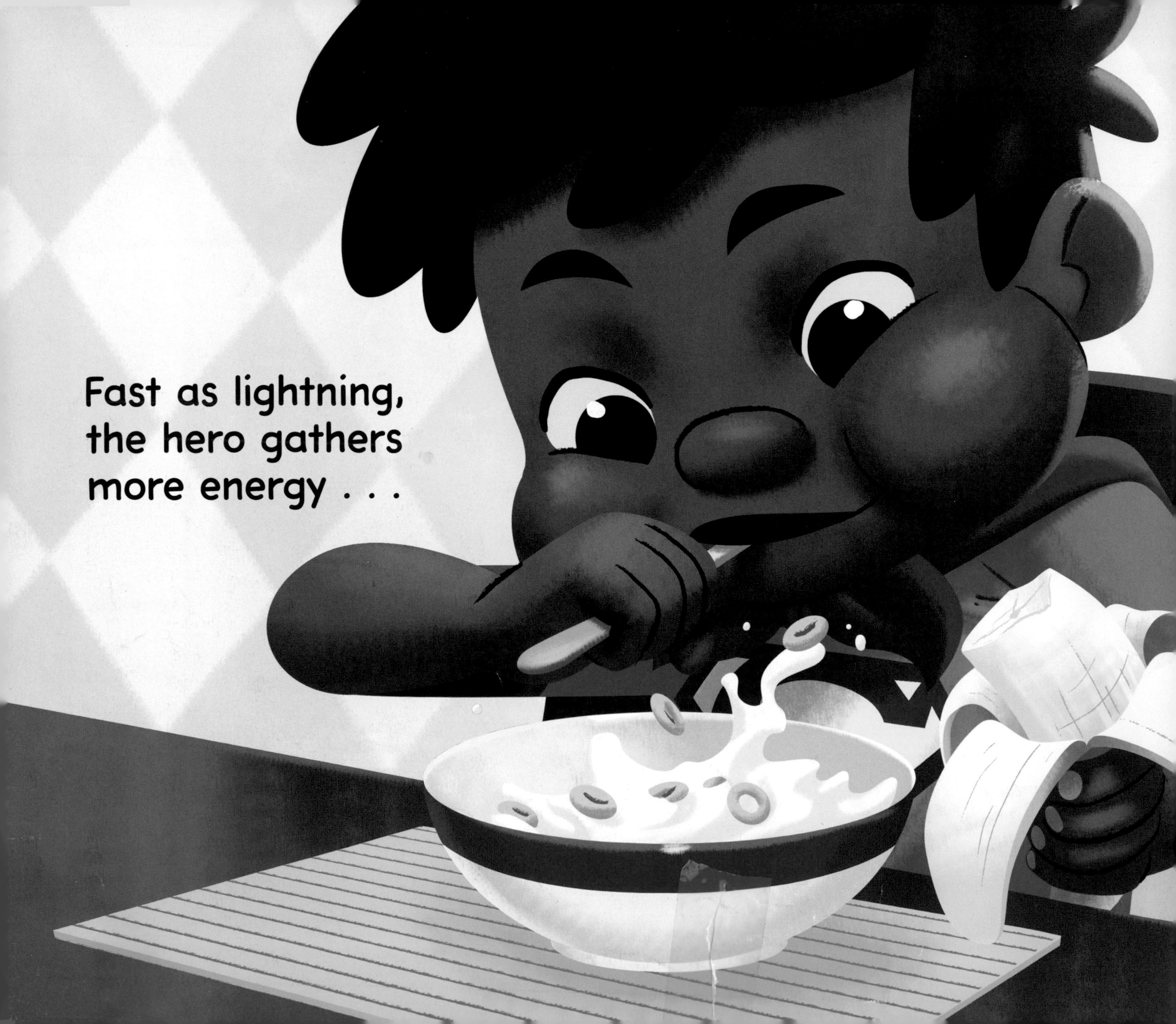

Fast as lightning,
the hero gathers
more energy . . .

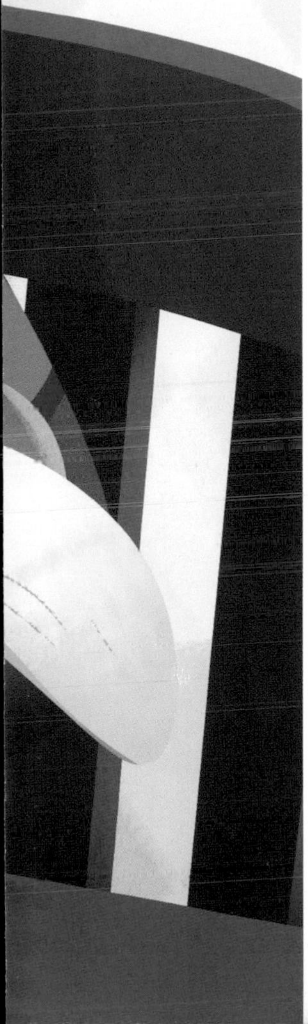

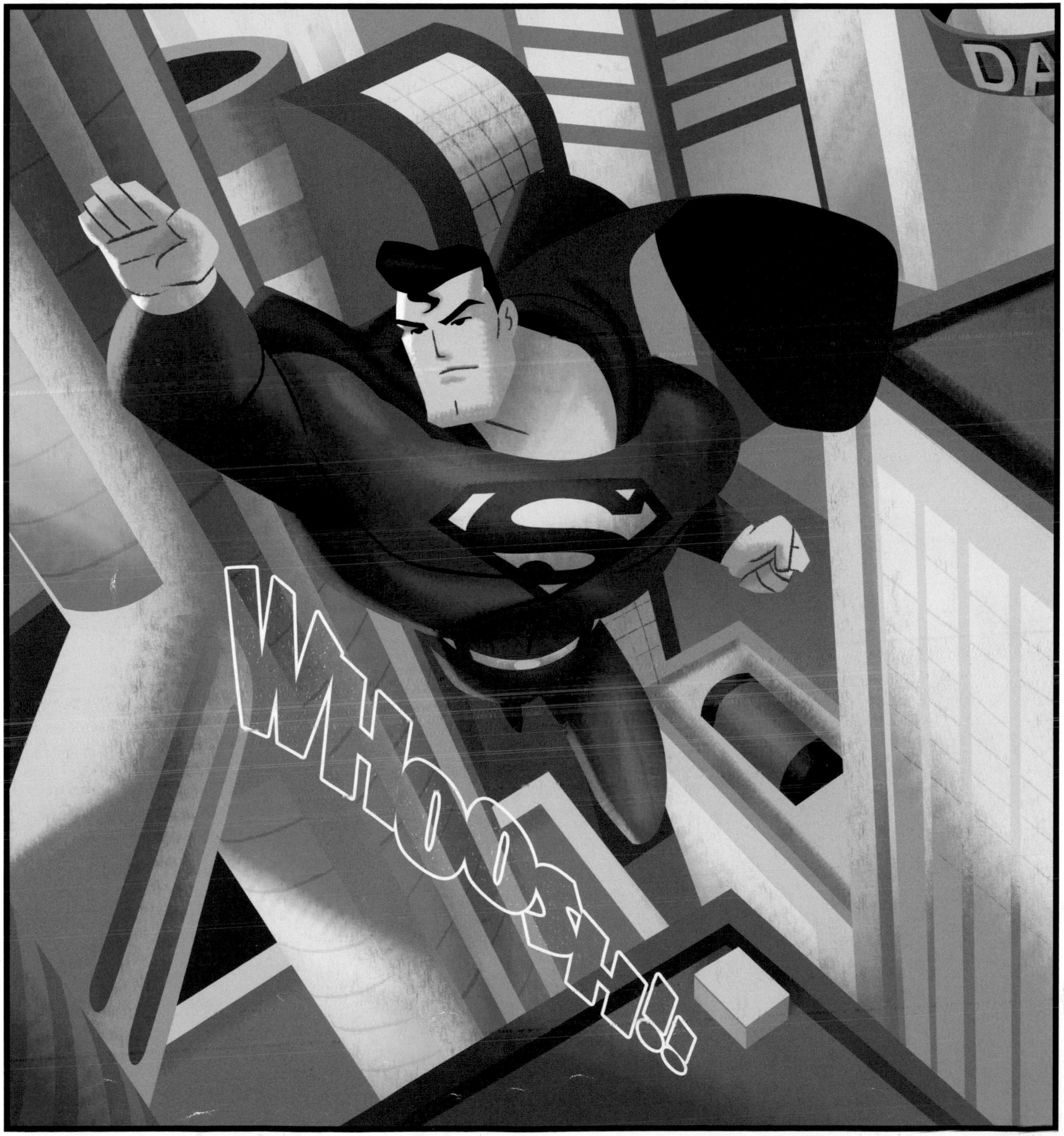
WHOOSH!!

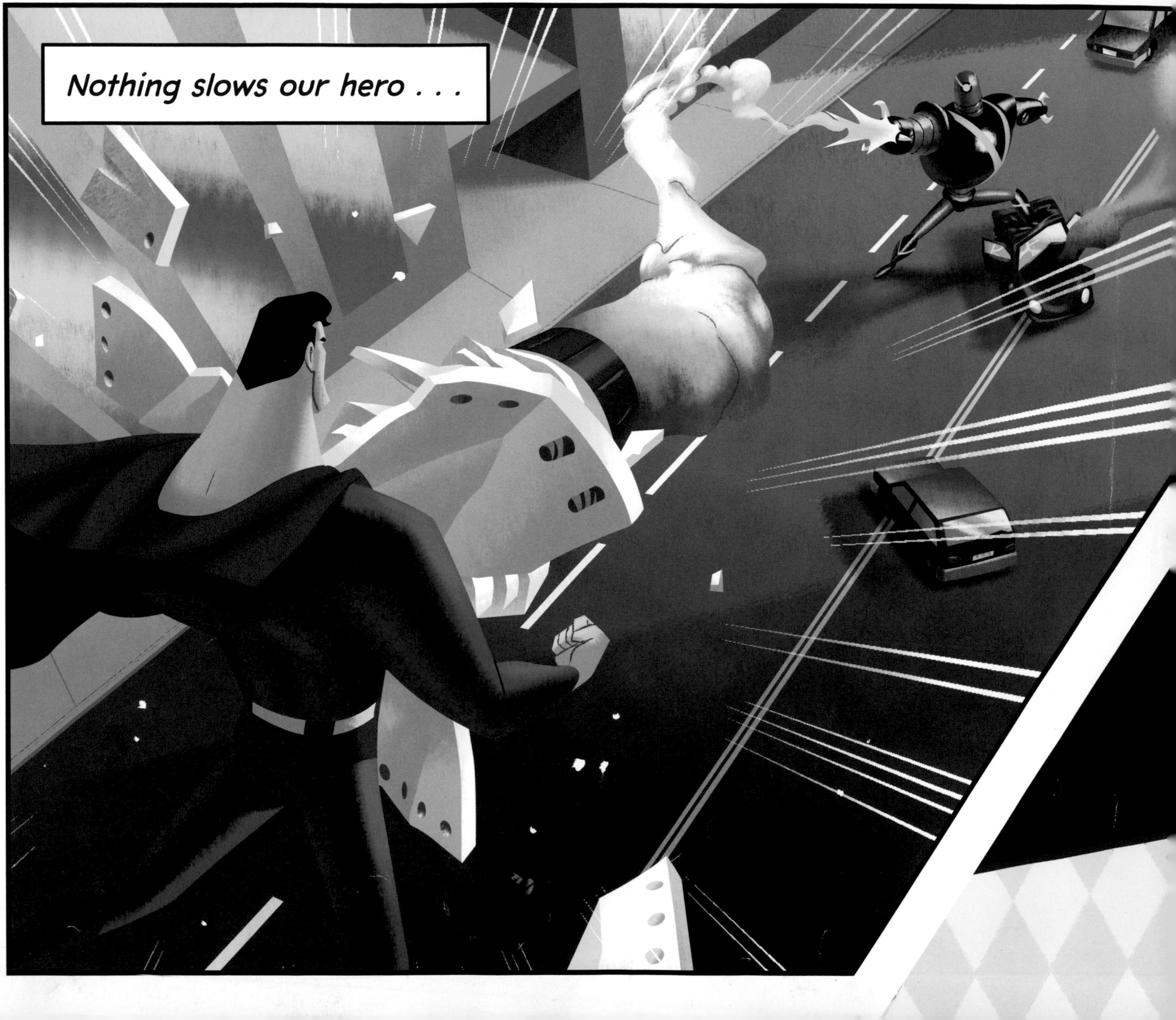
Nothing slows our hero . . .

. . . when he's on a mission!

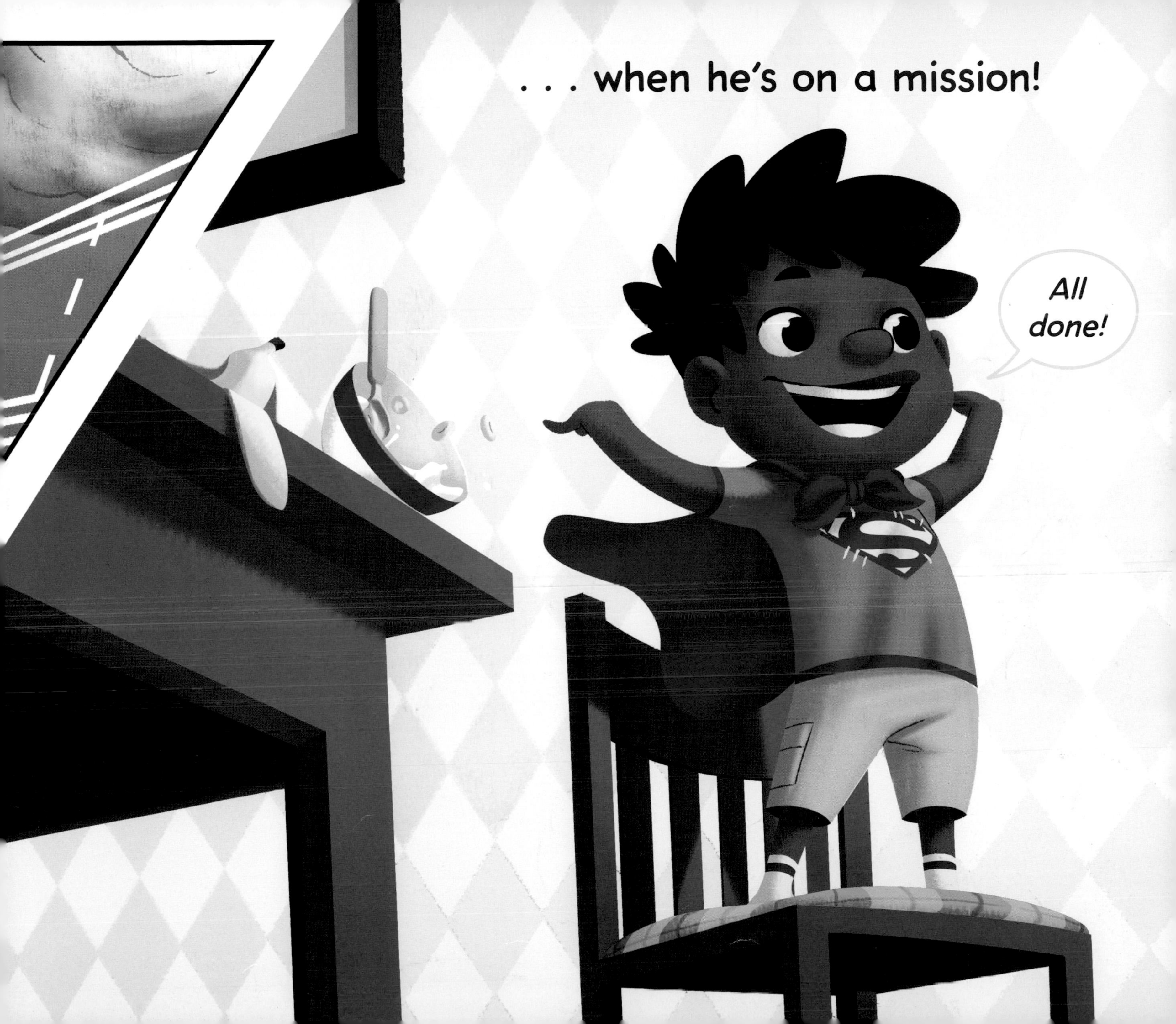
All done!

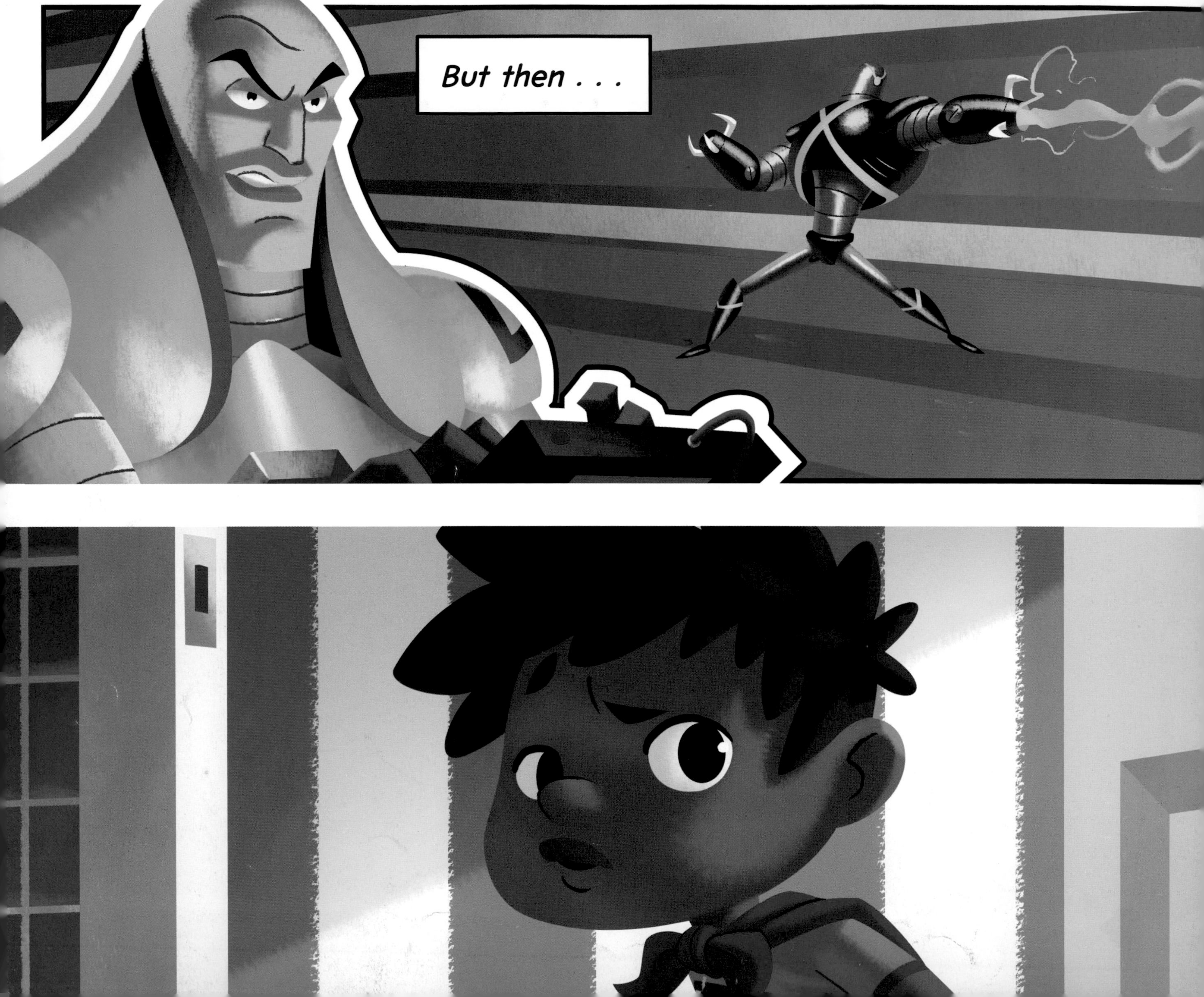
But then . . .

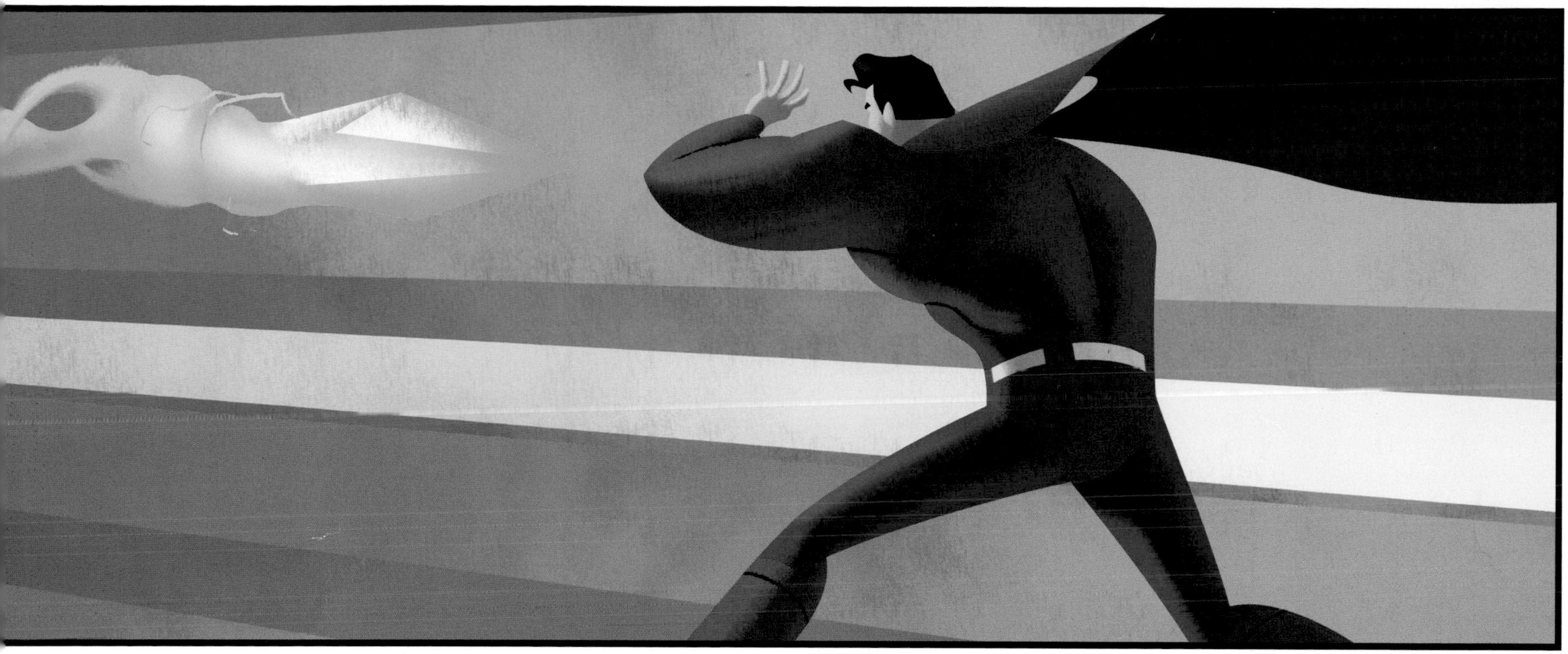

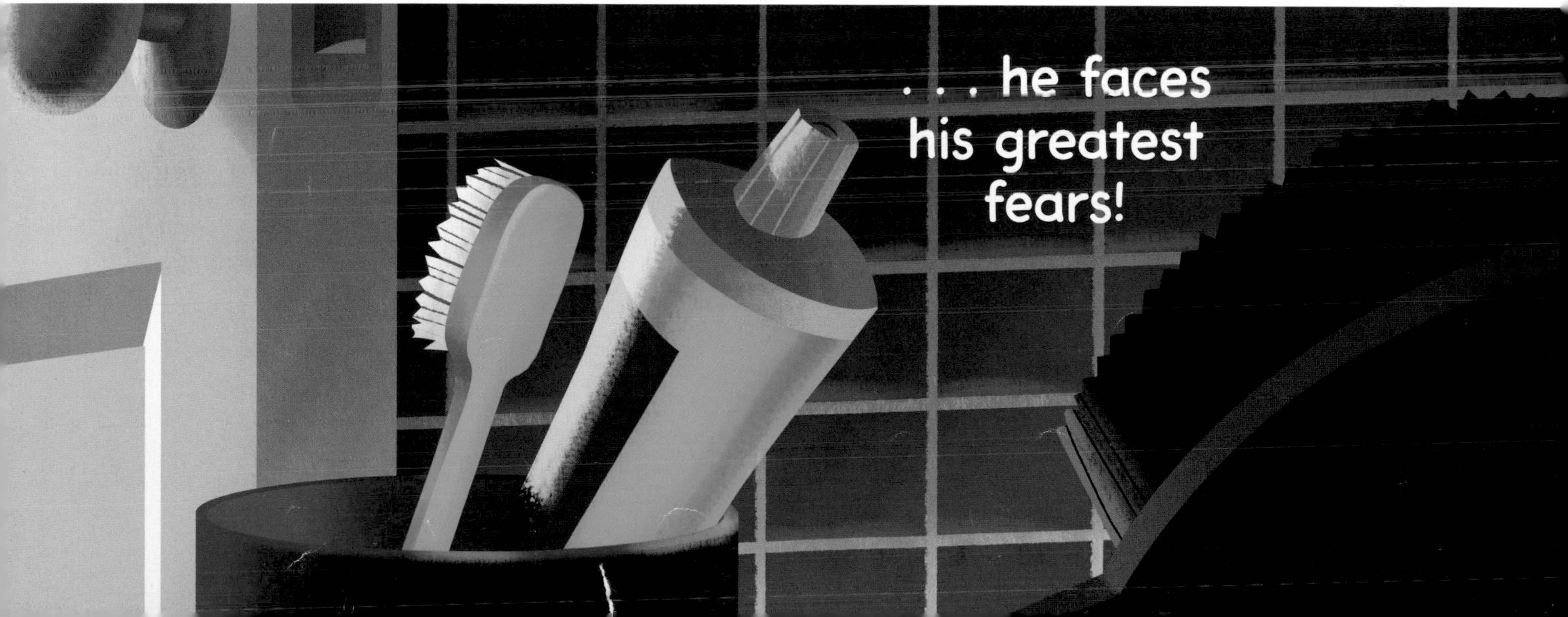
. . . he faces
his greatest
fears!

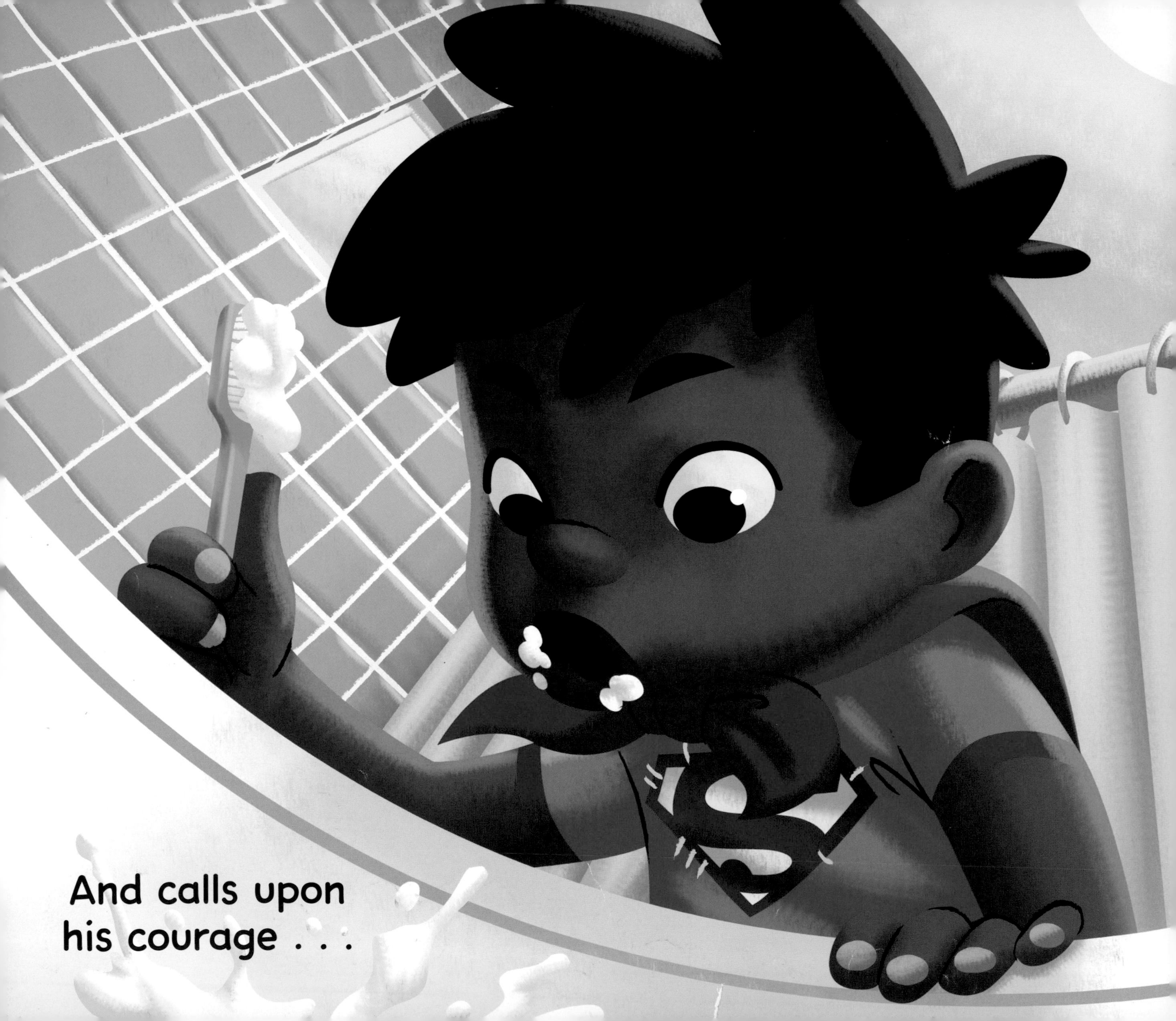

And calls upon
his courage . . .

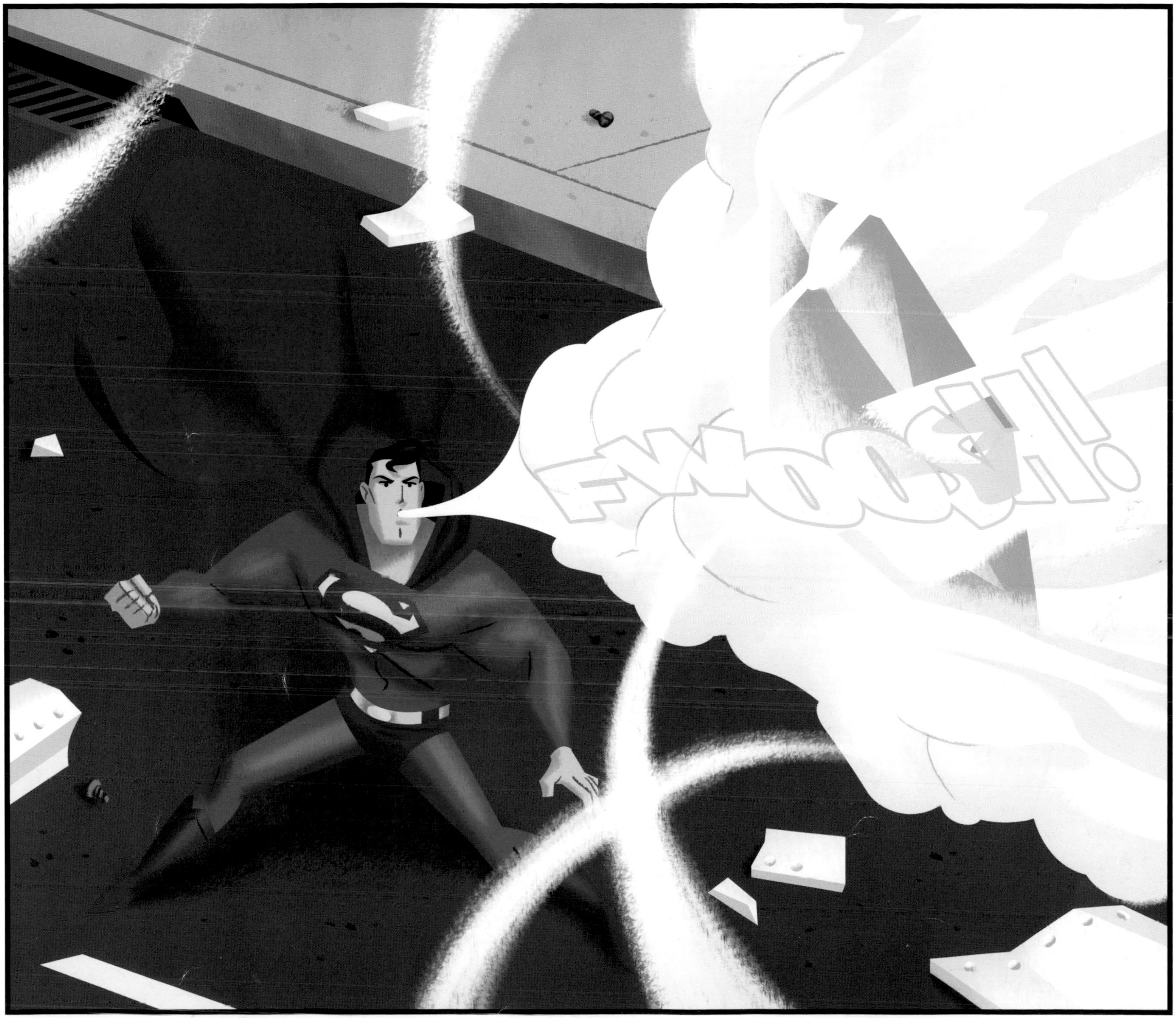
FWOOSH!!

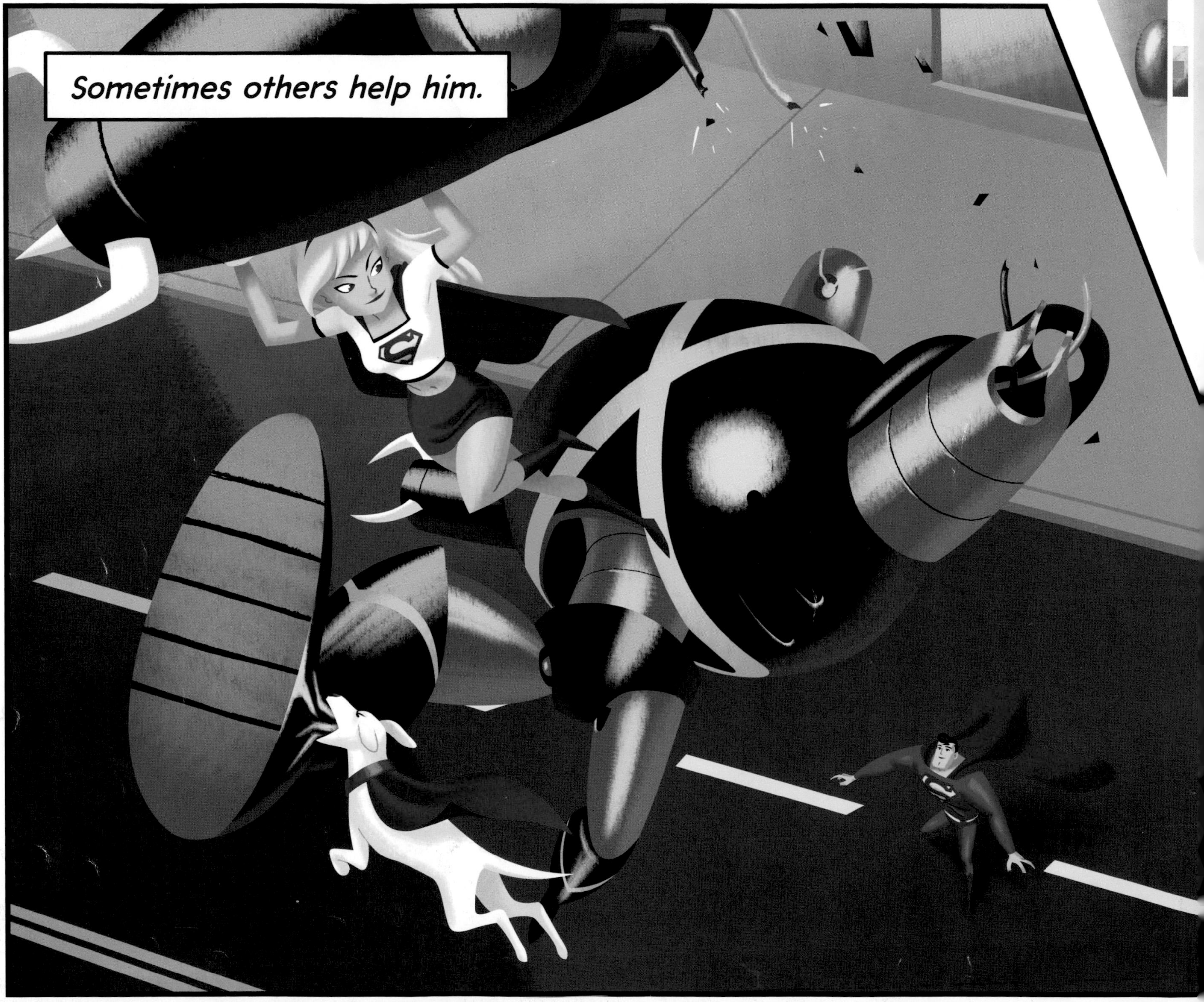
Sometimes others help him.

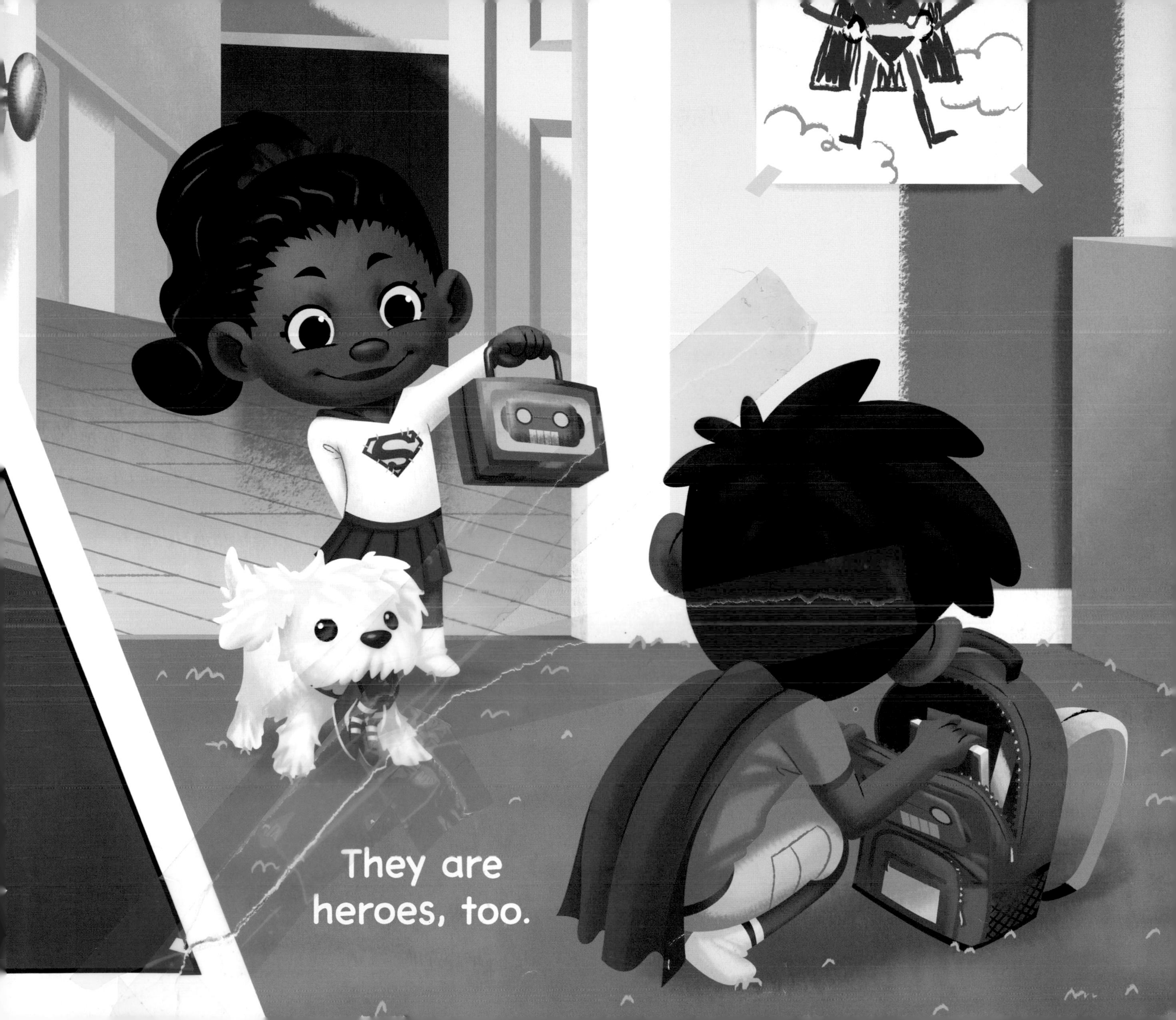

They are
heroes, too.

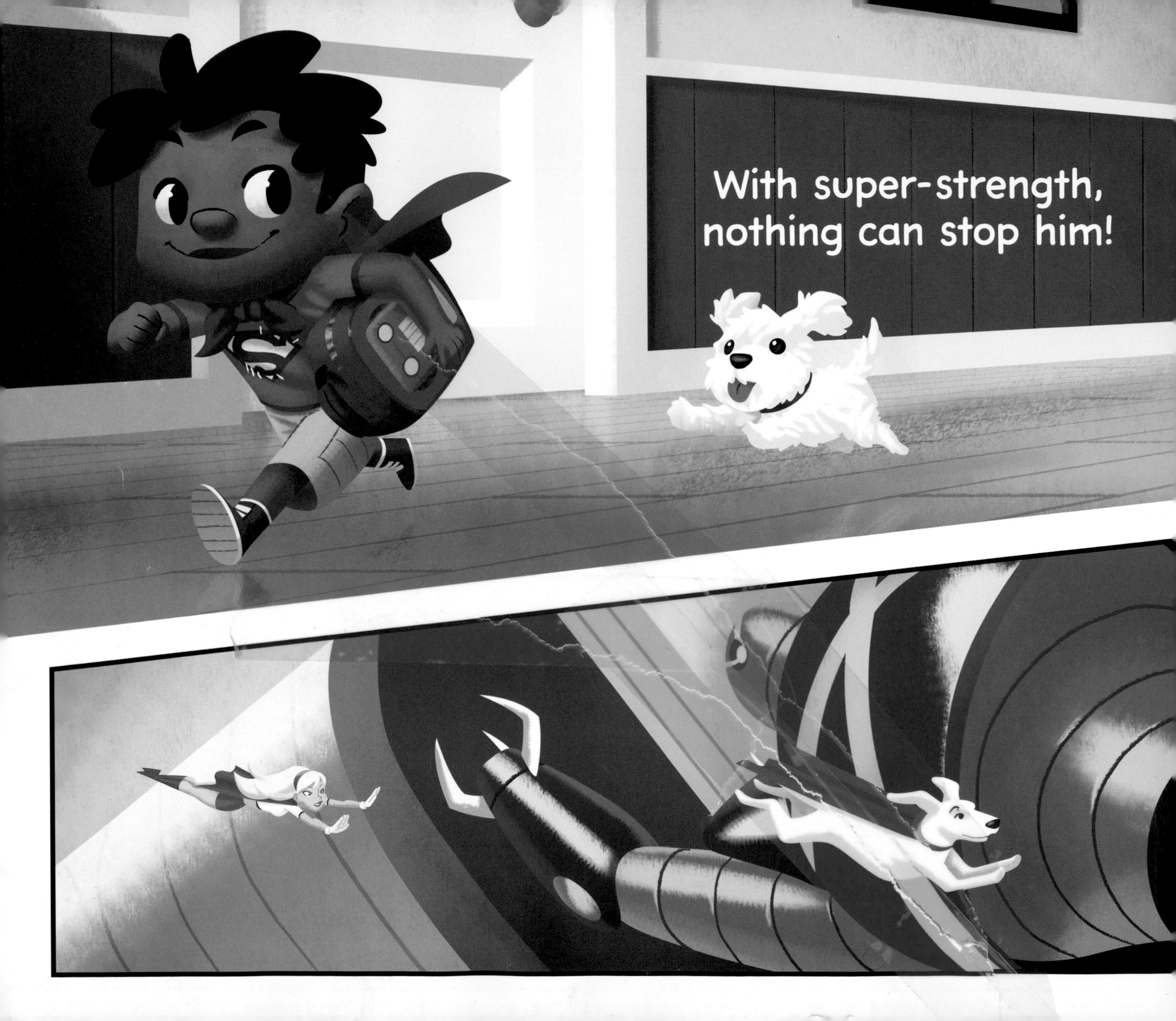
With super-strength, nothing can stop him!

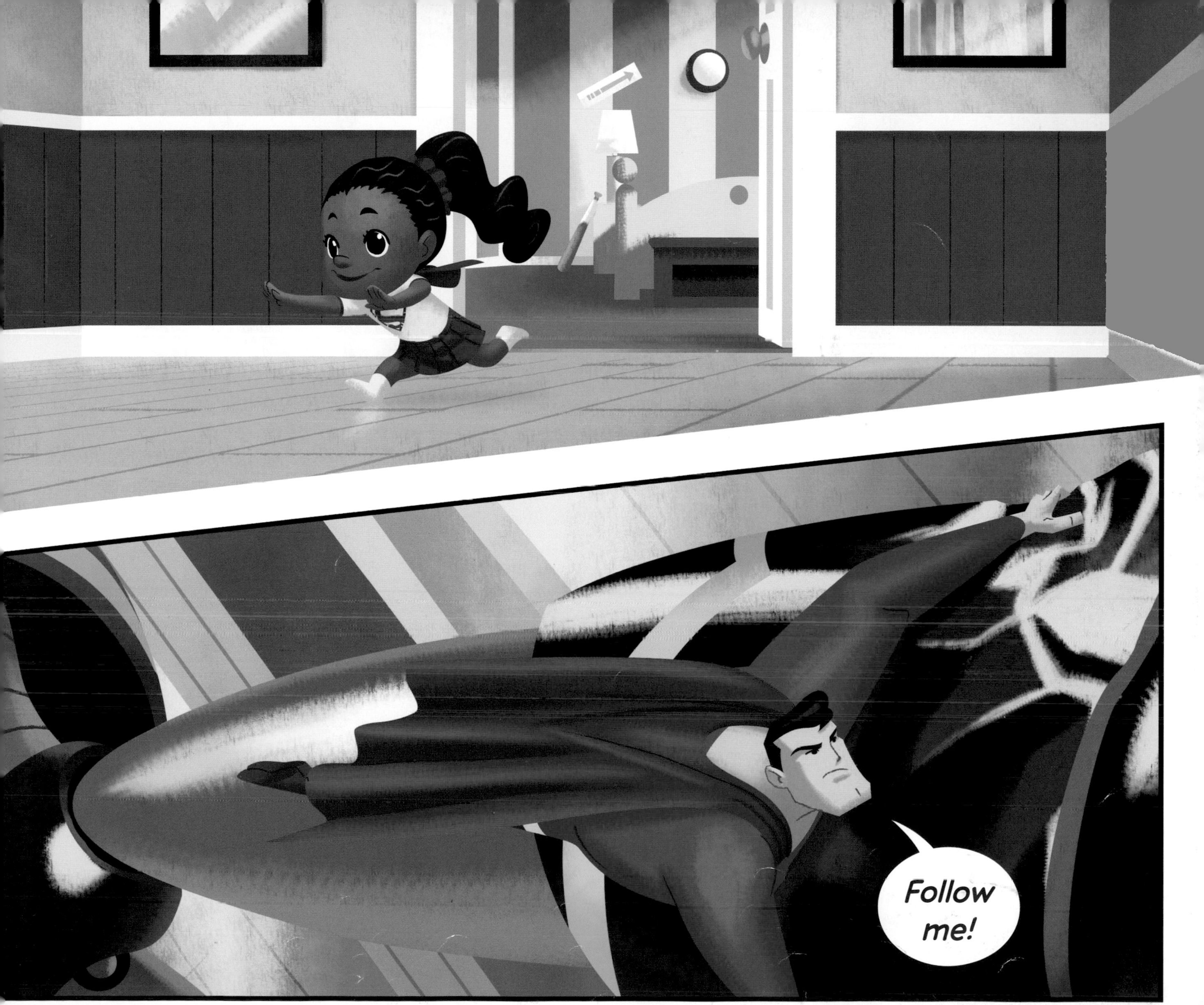
Follow me!

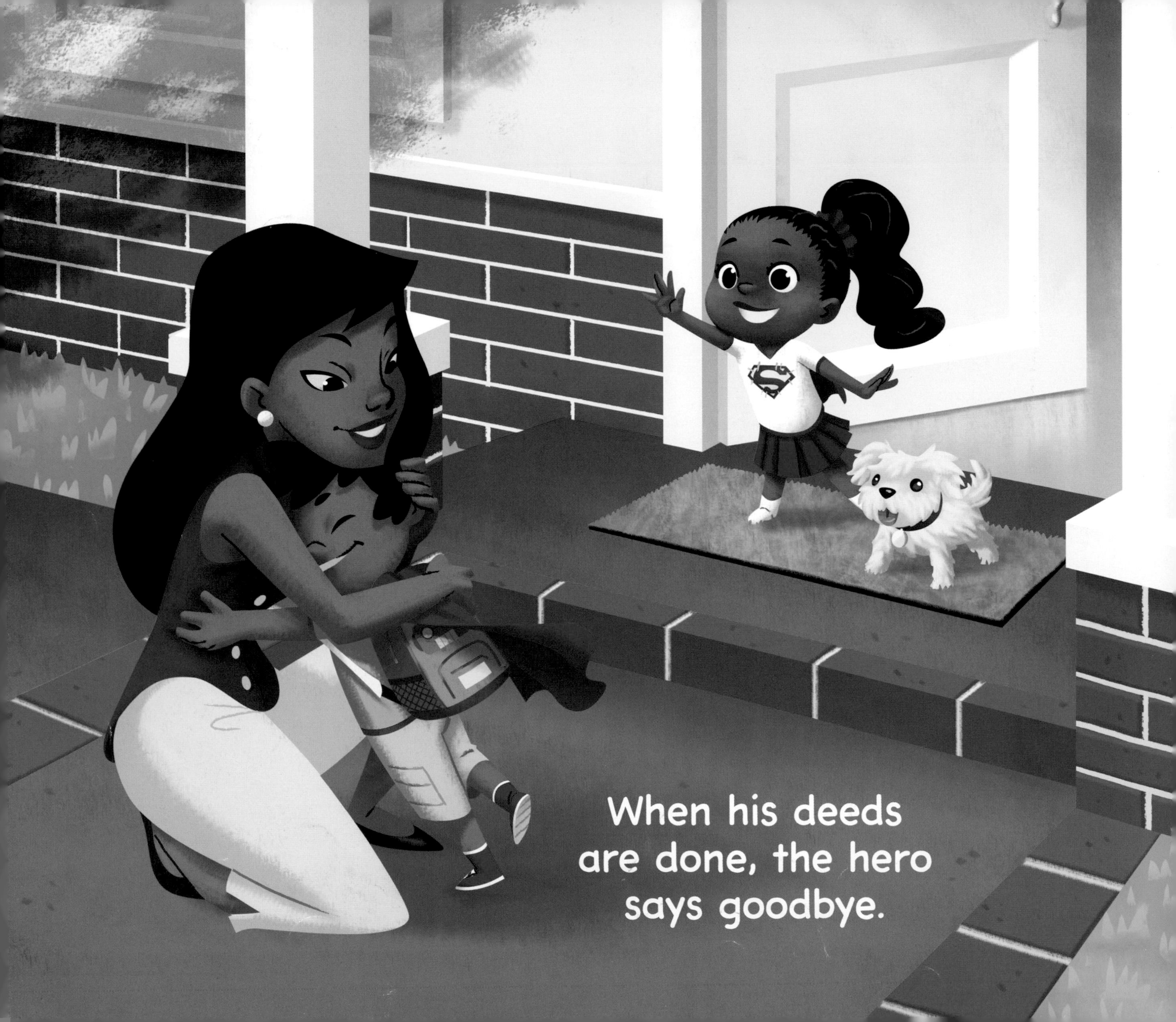

When his deeds are done, the hero says goodbye.

Then,
in a single
bound . . .

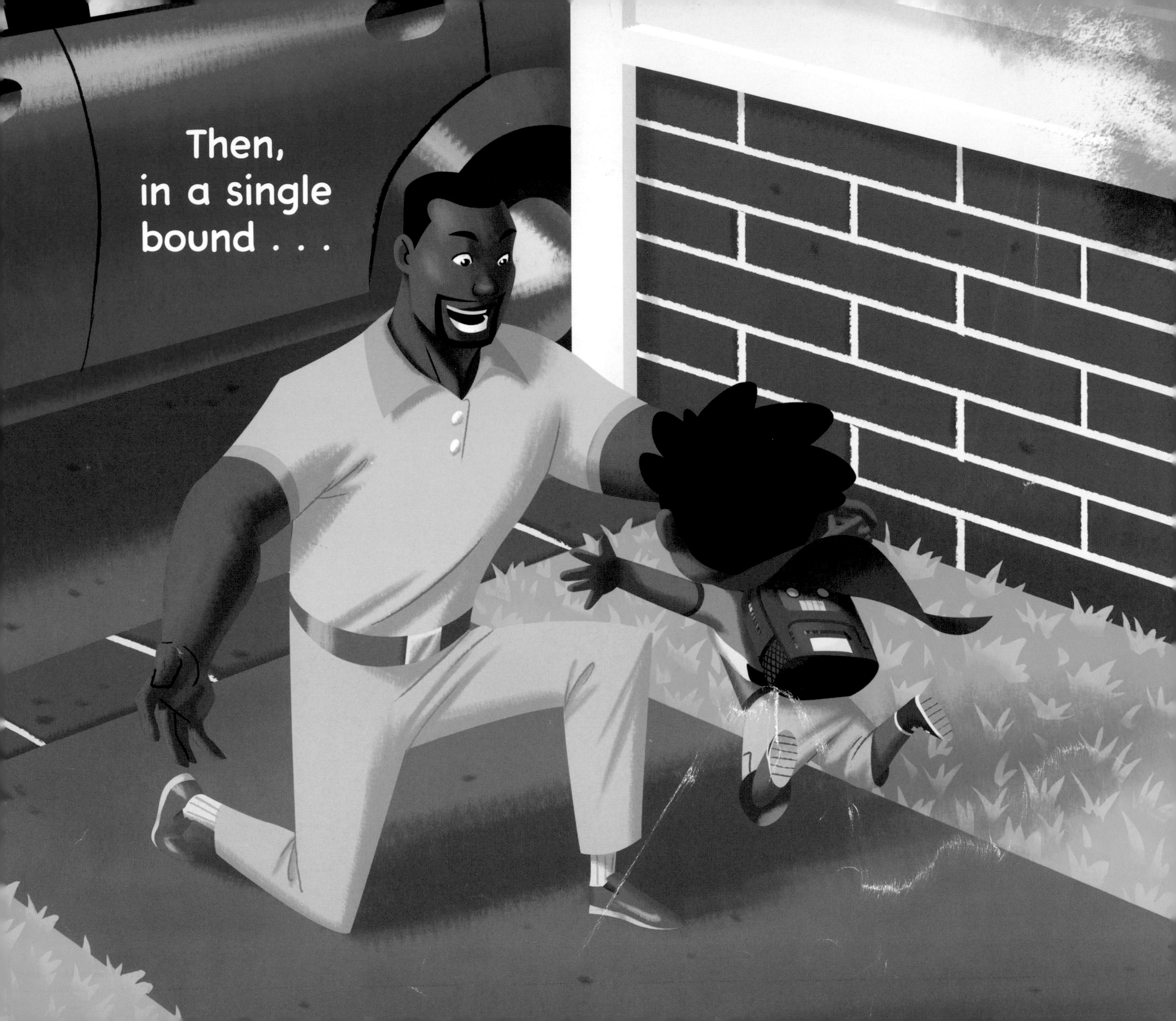

. . . the hero is up and away!

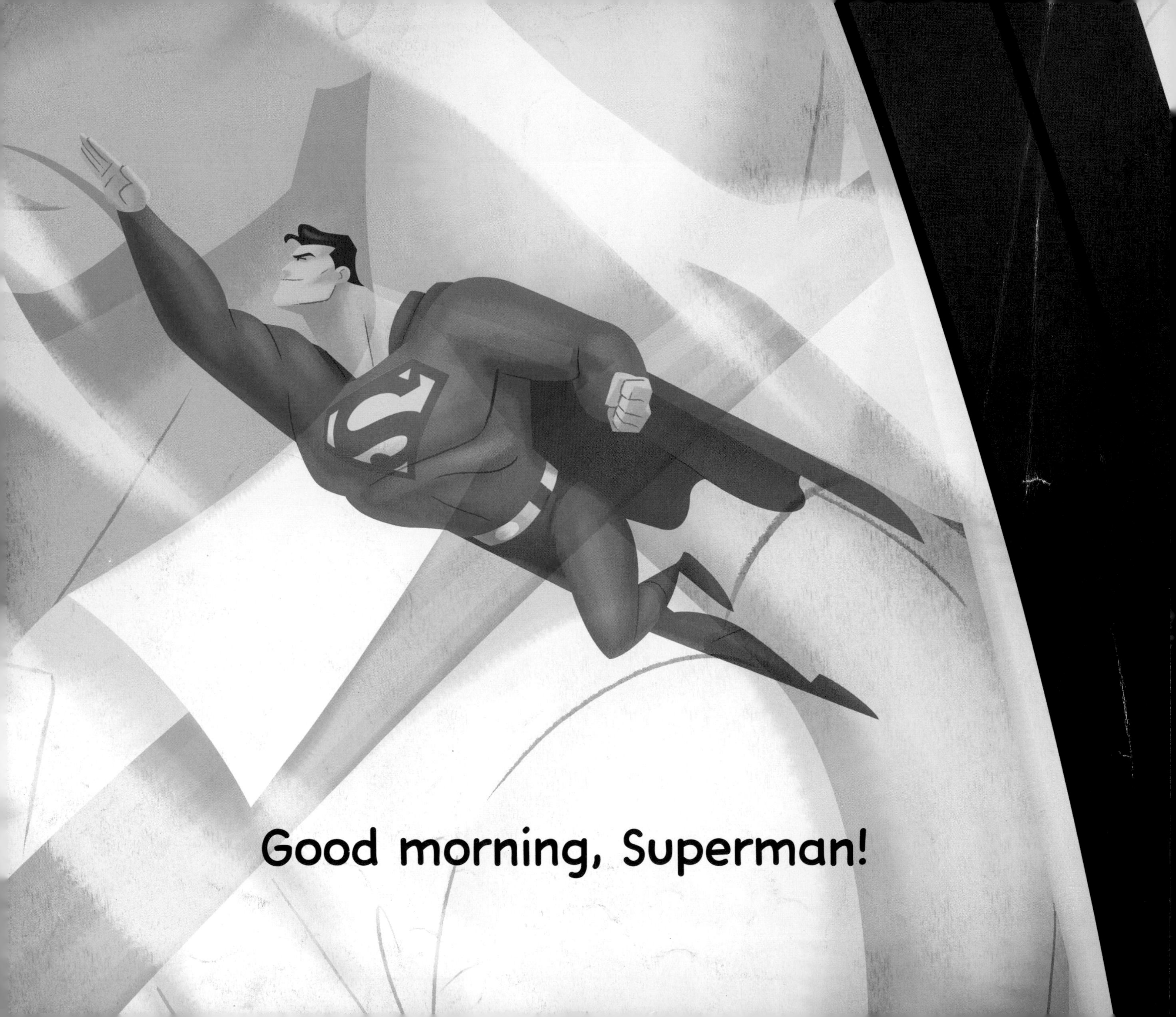

Good morning, Superman!

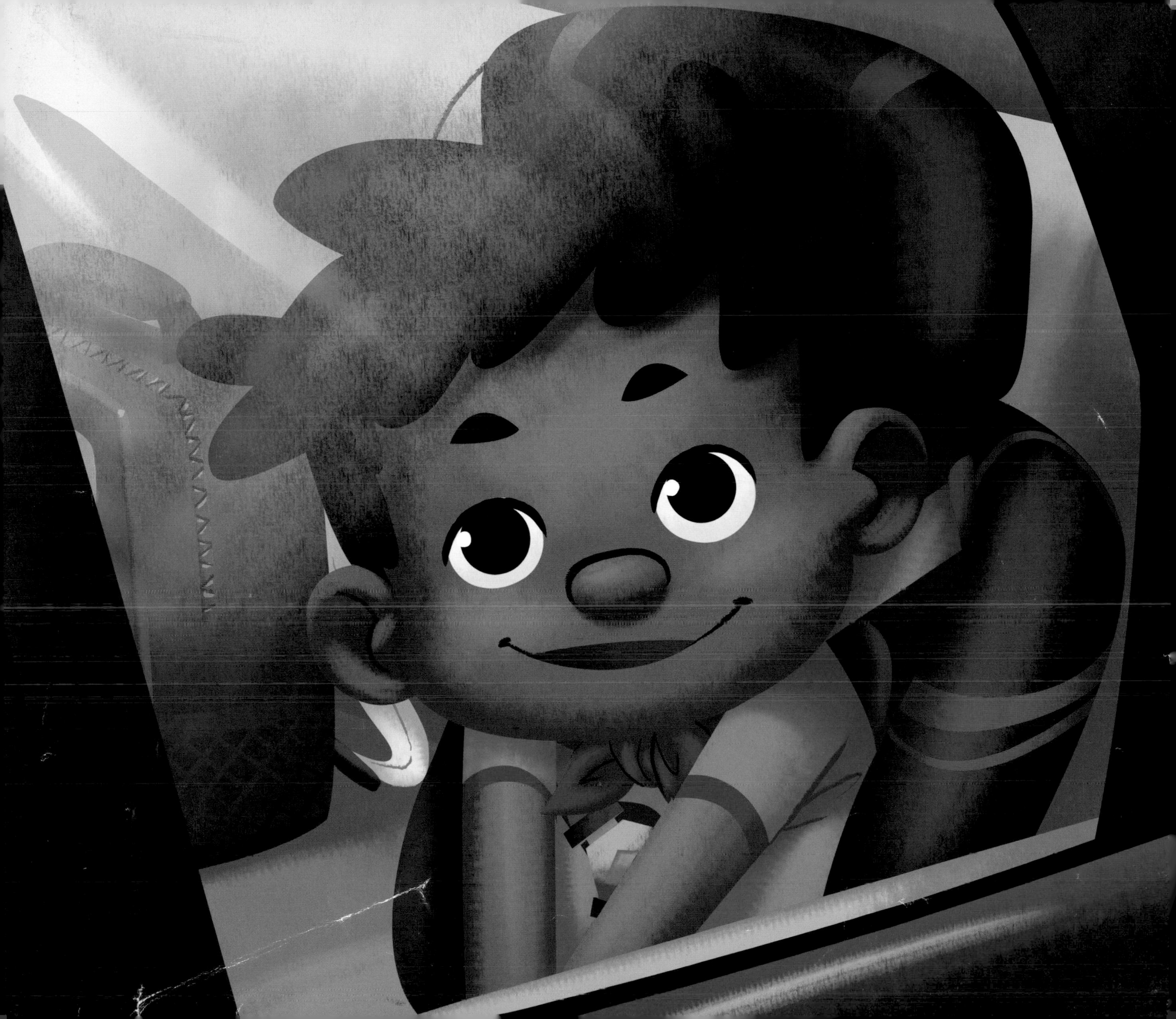

MORNING CHECKLIST!

Go potty

Get dressed

Eat breakfast

Brush teeth

Pack bag

Hugs and kisses